Frankie

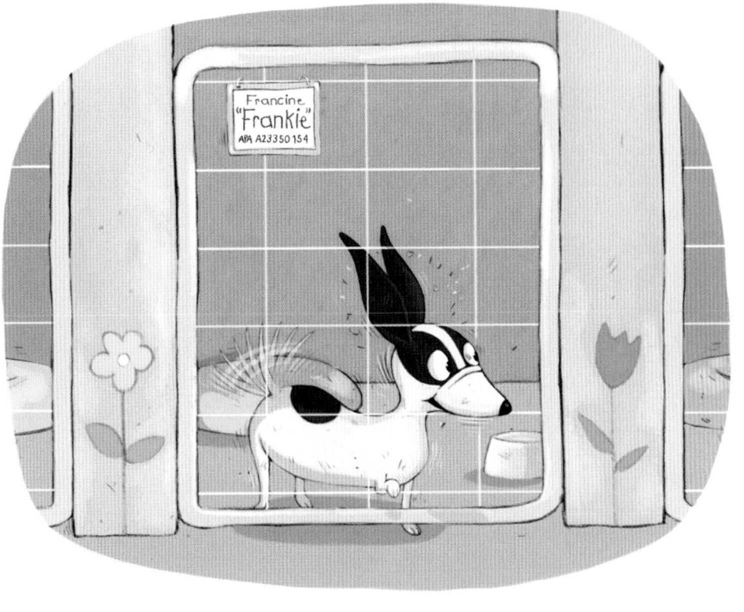
Francine
"Frankie"
APA A23350154

Words and pictures by Mary Sullivan

HOUGHTON MIFFLIN HARCOURT
Boston New York

To Austin Pets Alive,
for helping me get Frankie
all buttoned up and beautiful
and ready for her forever home.

~ and ~

To Sue, Leslie, Cali, and Barkley,
for adopting Frankie.
—M.S.

All rights reserved. For information about permission to reproduce selections from this book,
write to trade.permissions@hmhco.com or to Permissions, Houghton Mifflin Harcourt
Publishing Company, 3 Park Avenue, 19th Floor, New York, New York 10016.
www.hmhco.com

The text of this book is set in Bo Chen.
The illustrations are pencil on Strathmore drawing paper, scanned and digitally colored.

ISBN 978-0-544-61113-9

Manufactured in China
SCP 10 9 8 7 6 5 4 3 2 1
4500638601

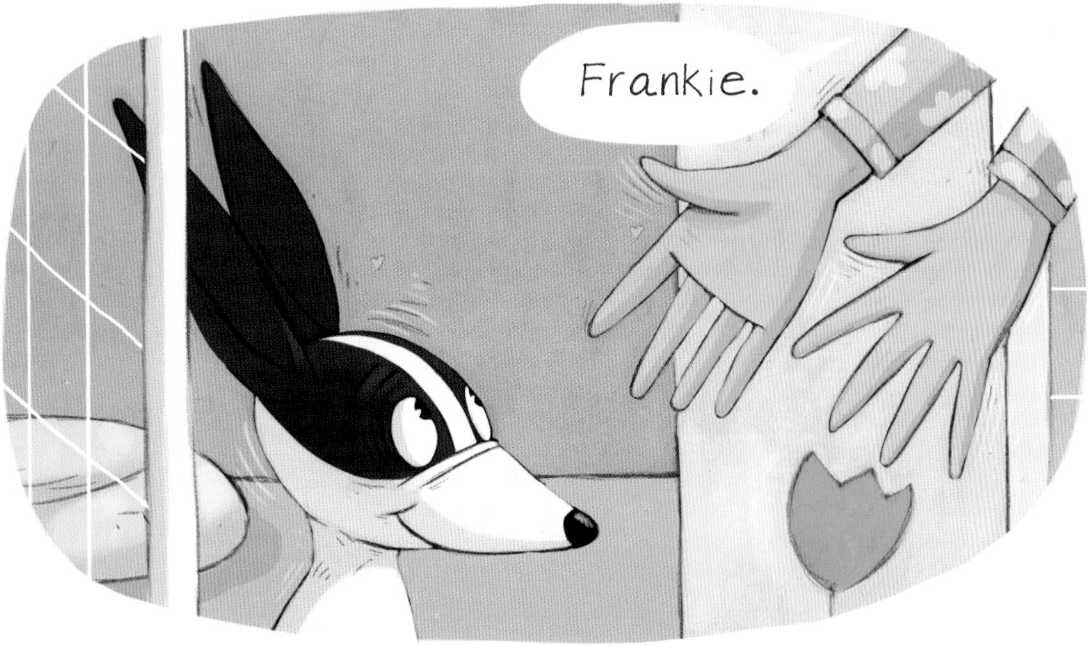
Frankie.

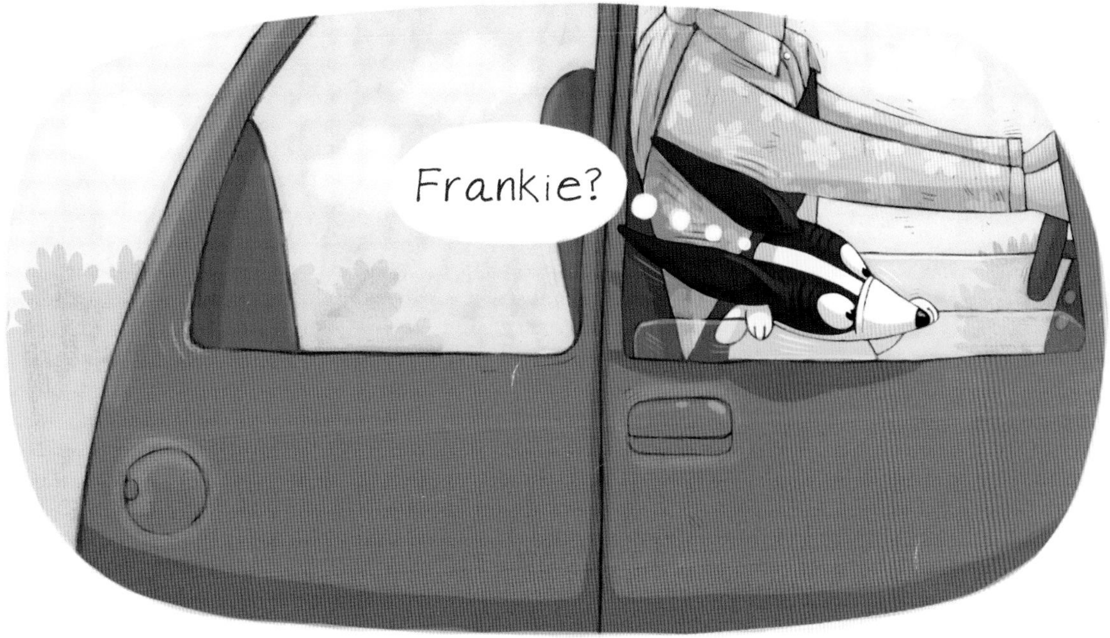
Frankie?

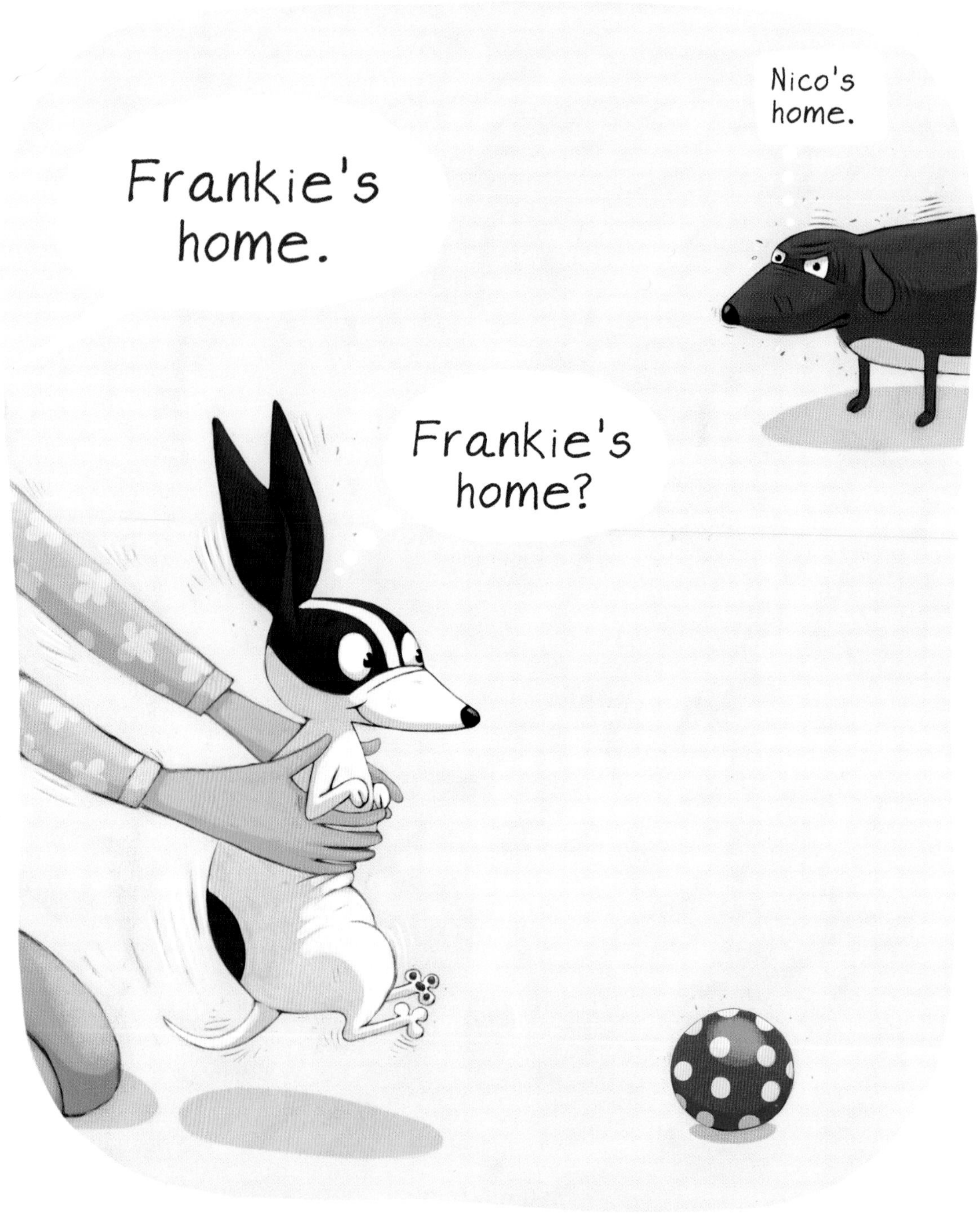
Nico's home.
Frankie's home.
Frankie's home?

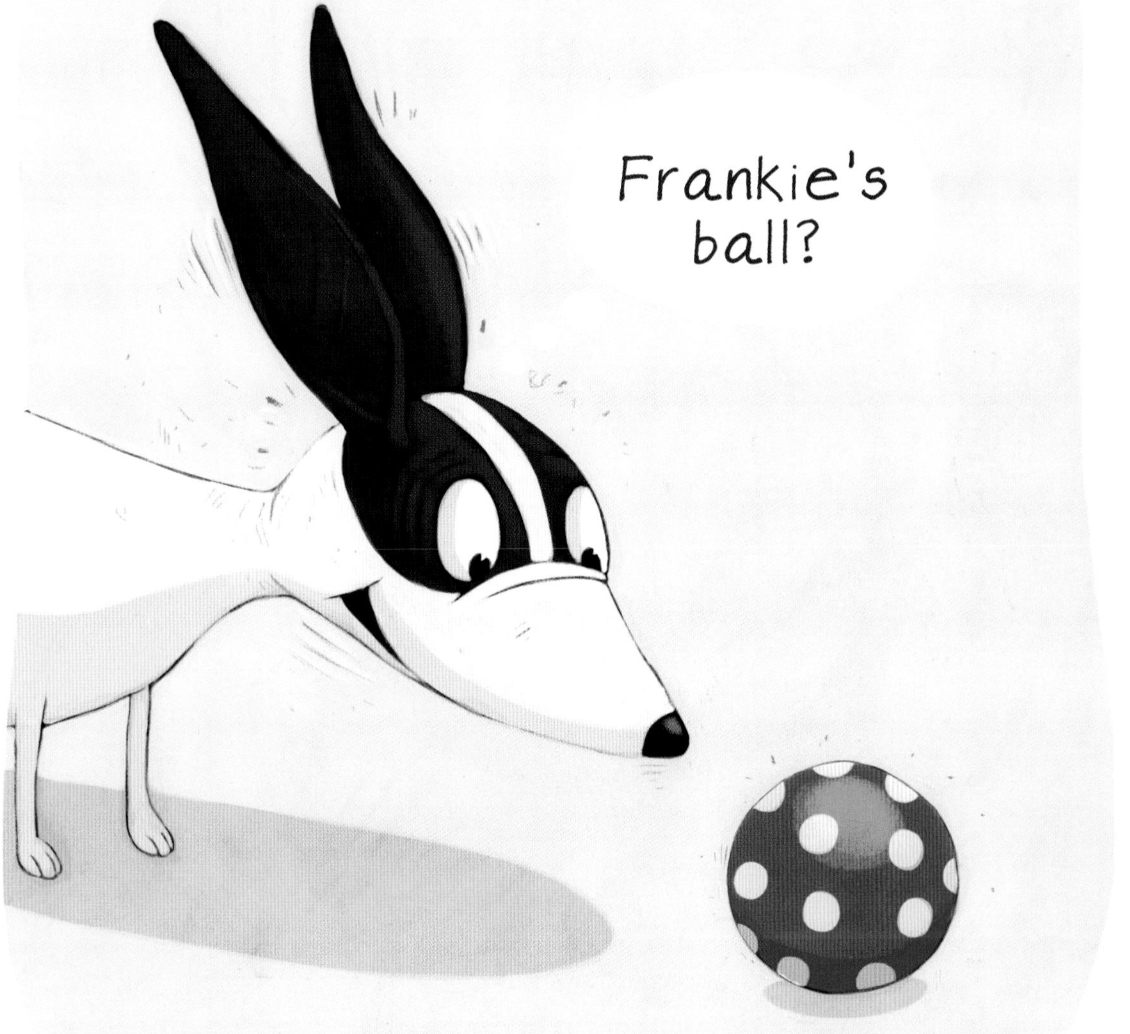
Frankie's ball?

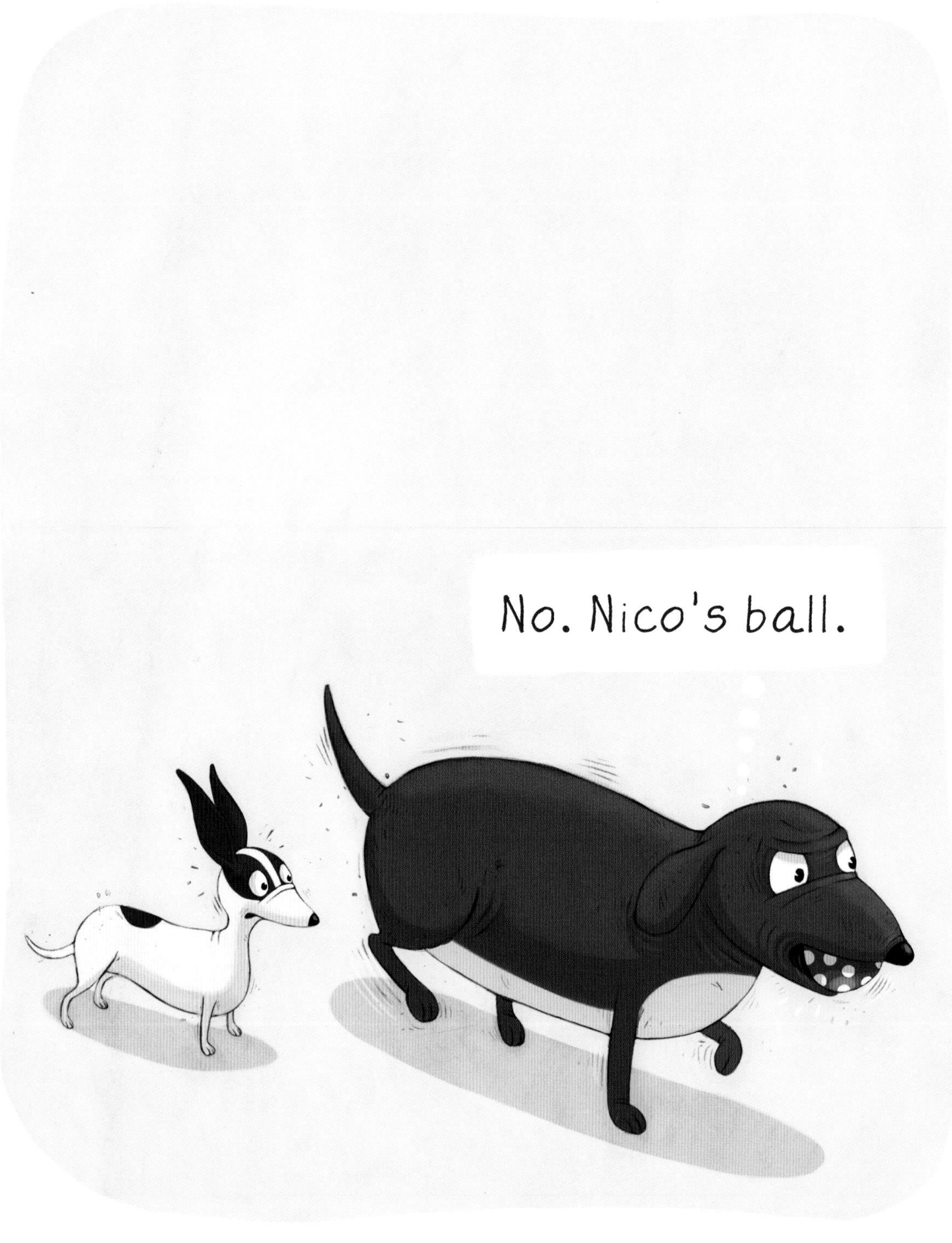
No. Nico's ball.

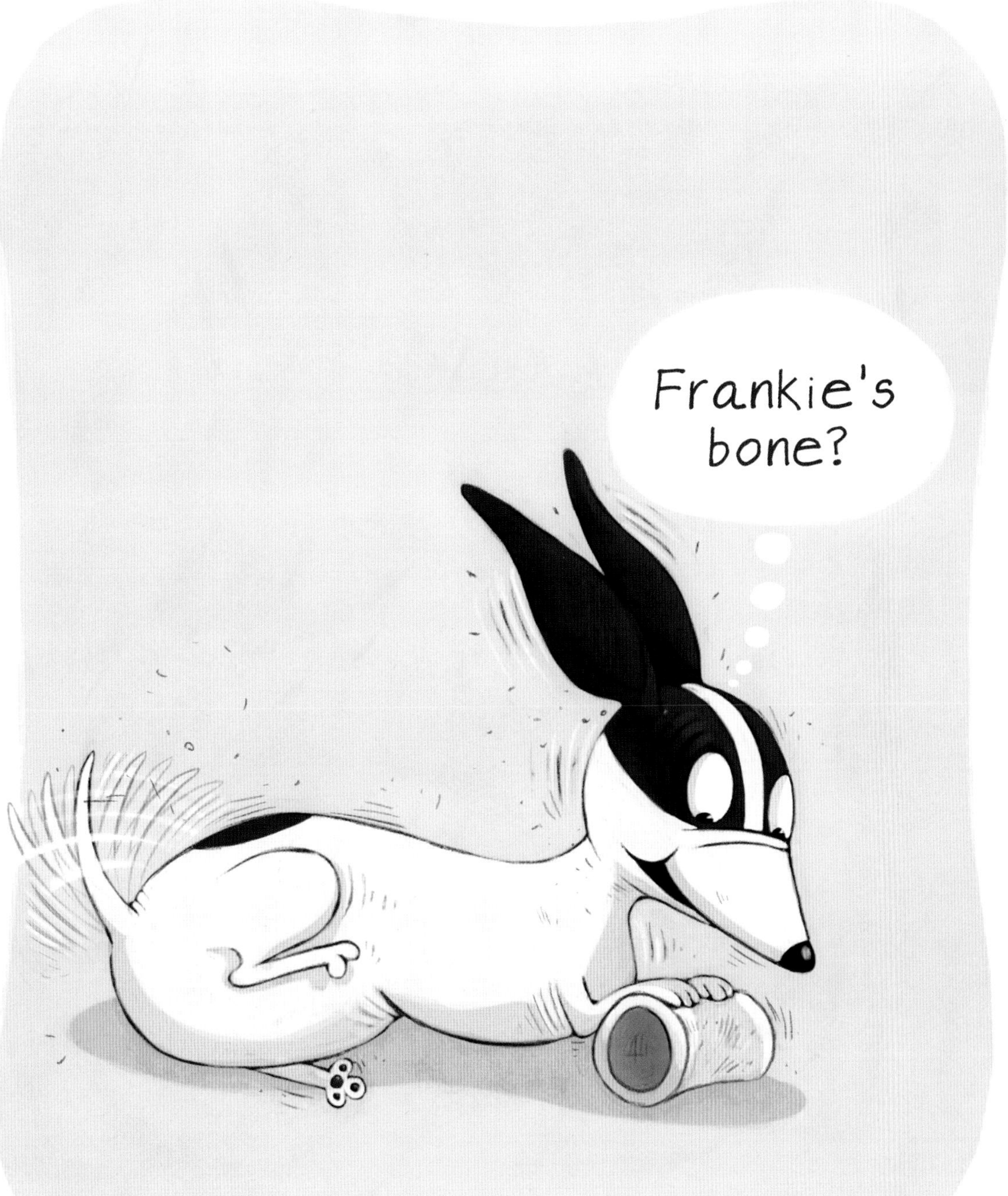
Frankie's
bone?

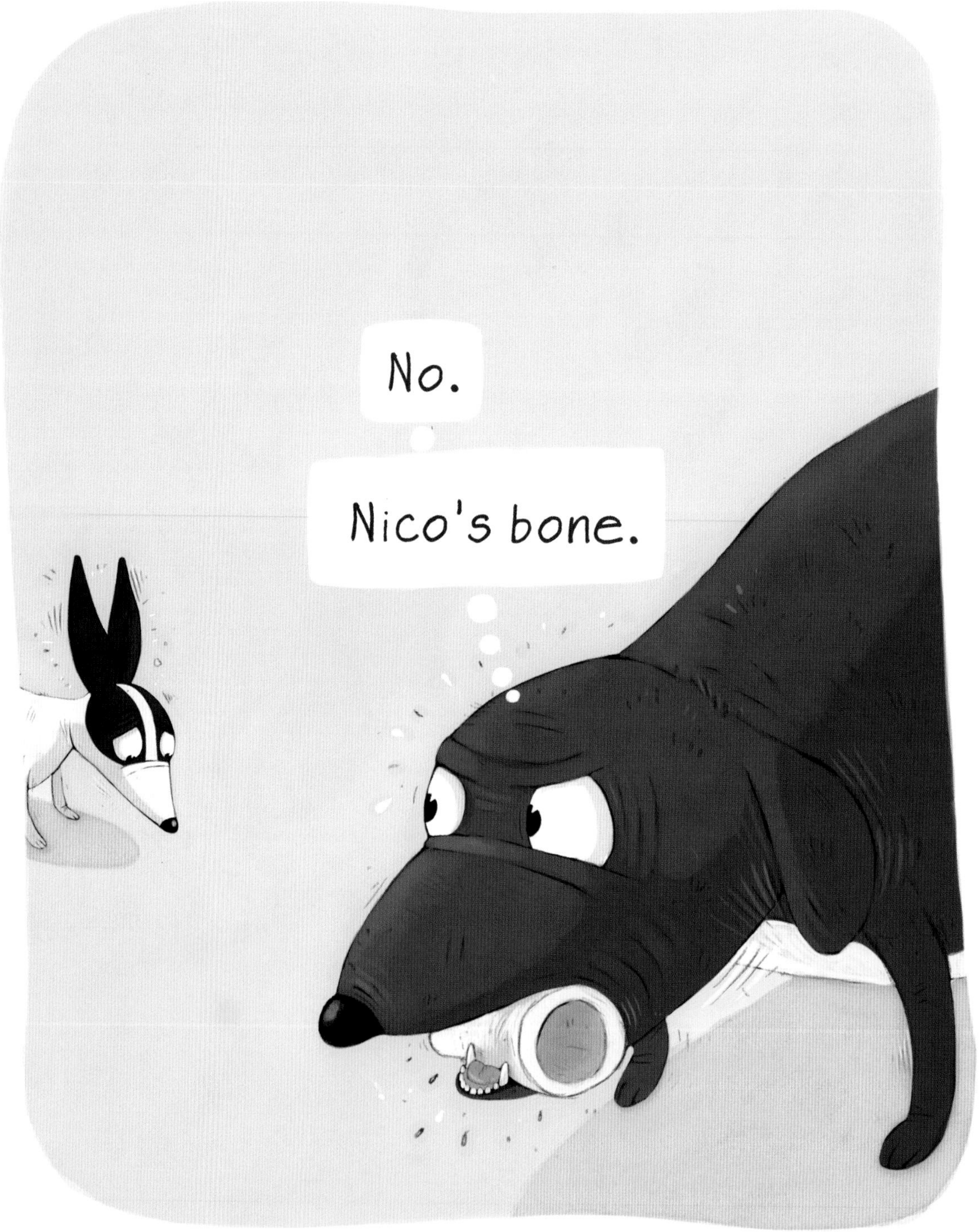
No.
Nico's bone.

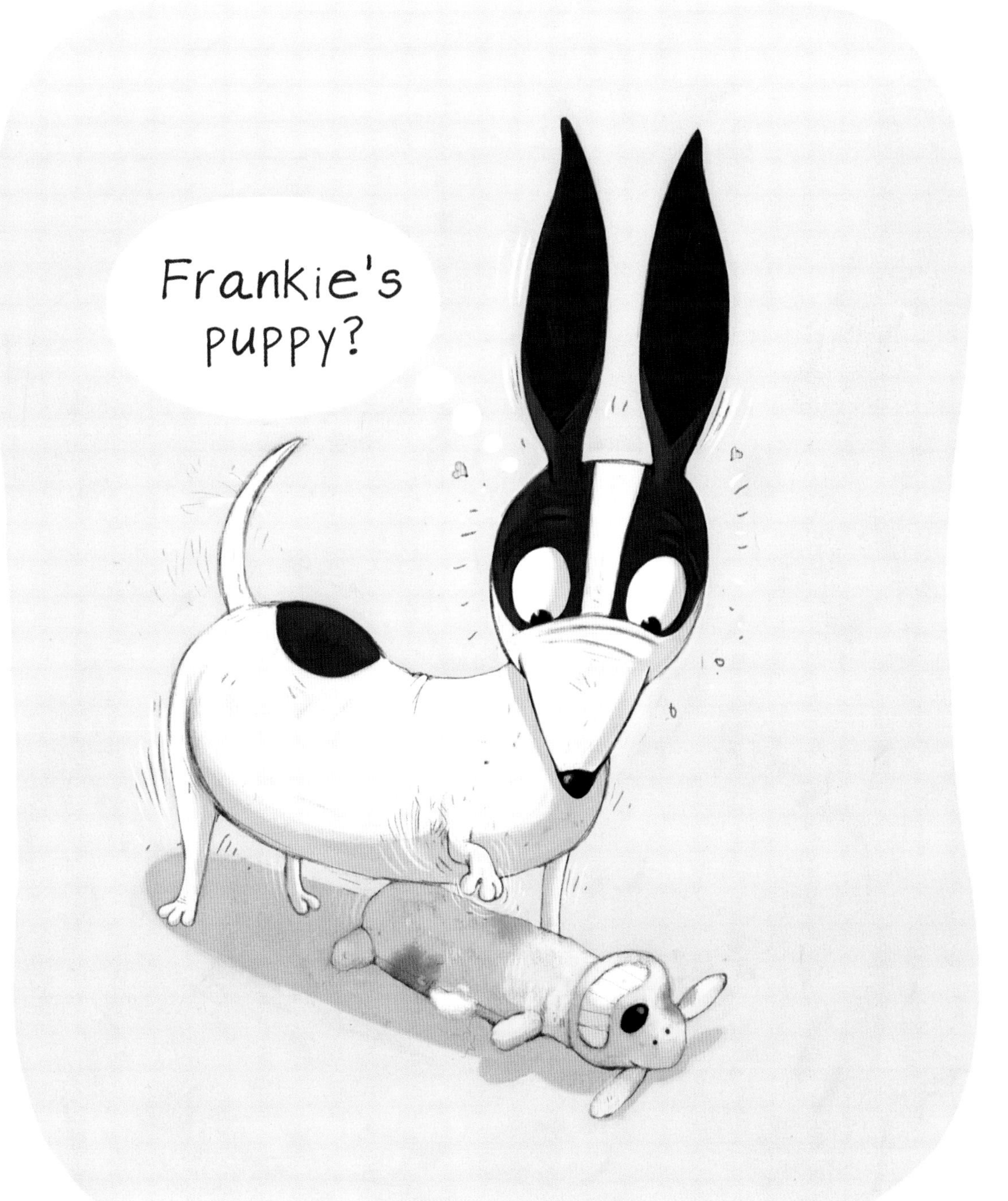
Frankie's
puppy?

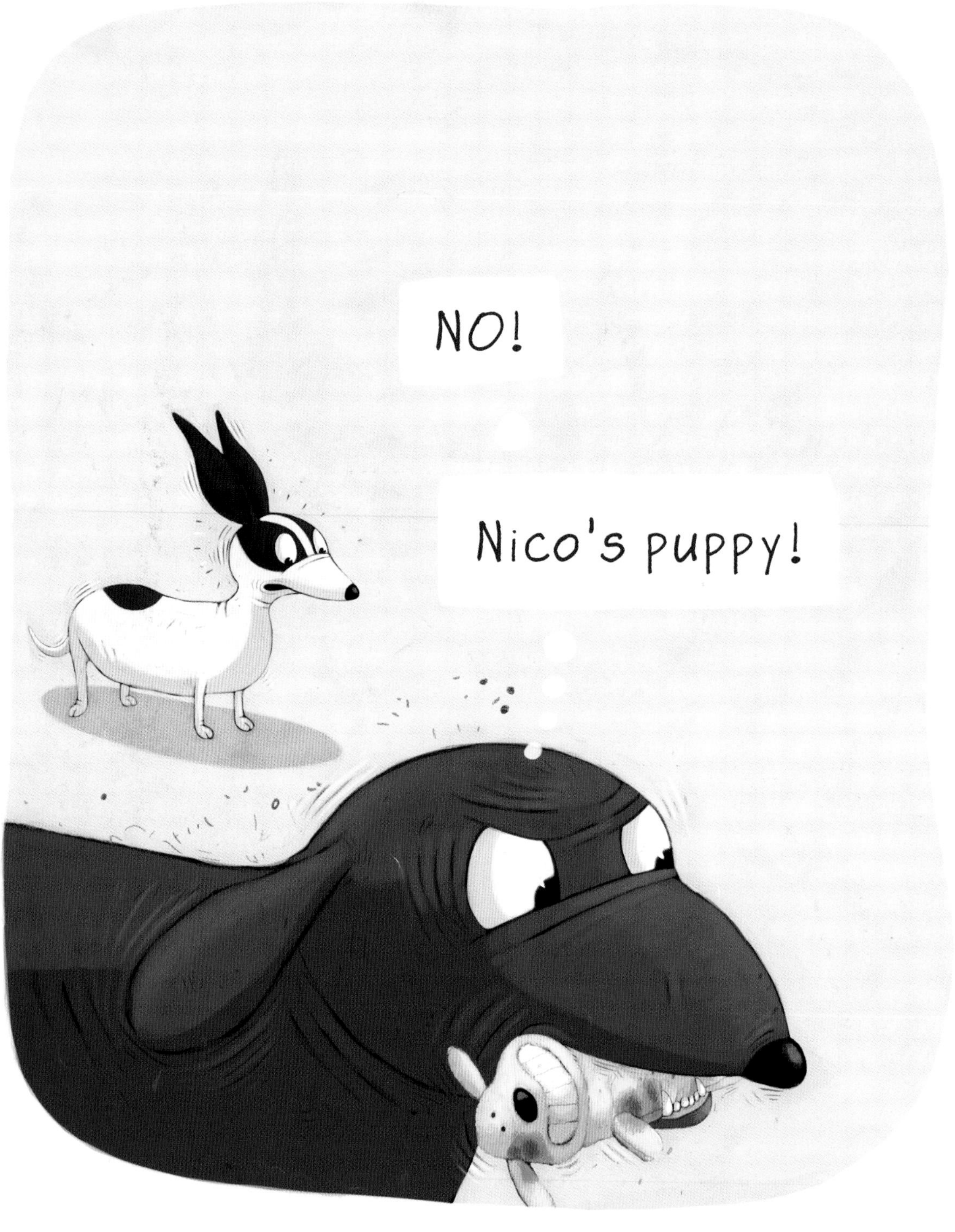
NO!
Nico's puppy!

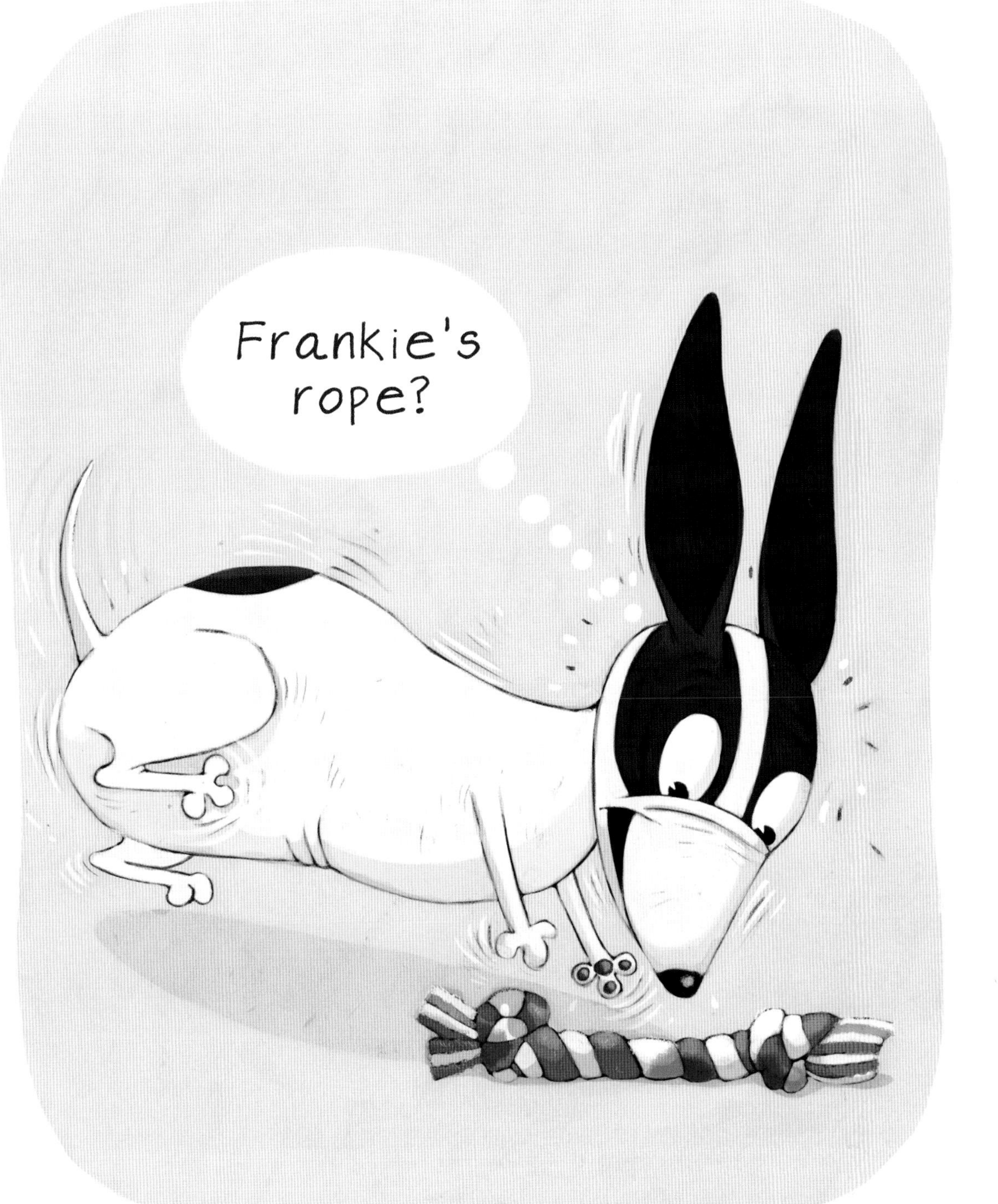
Frankie's
rope?

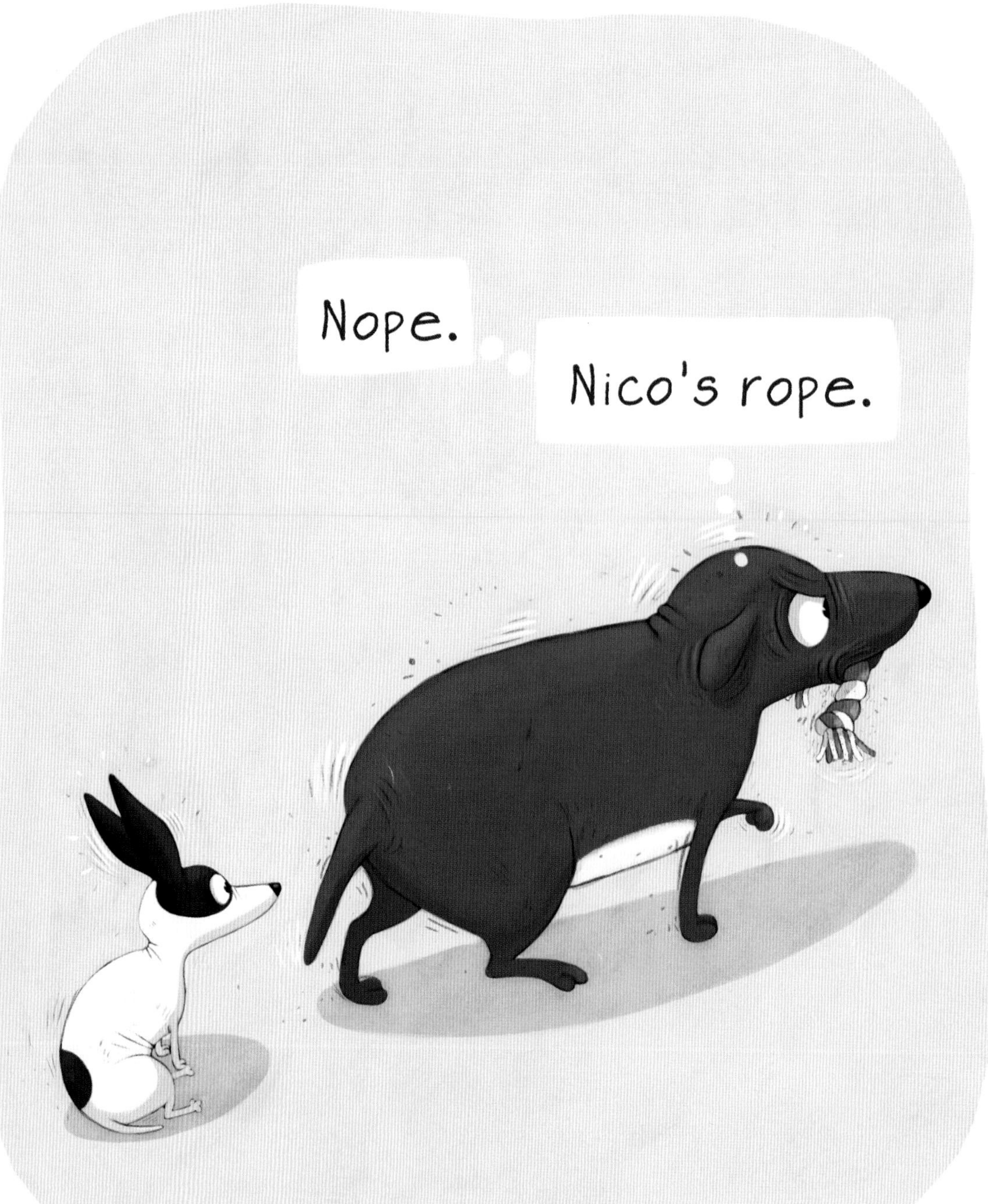
Nope.
Nico's rope.

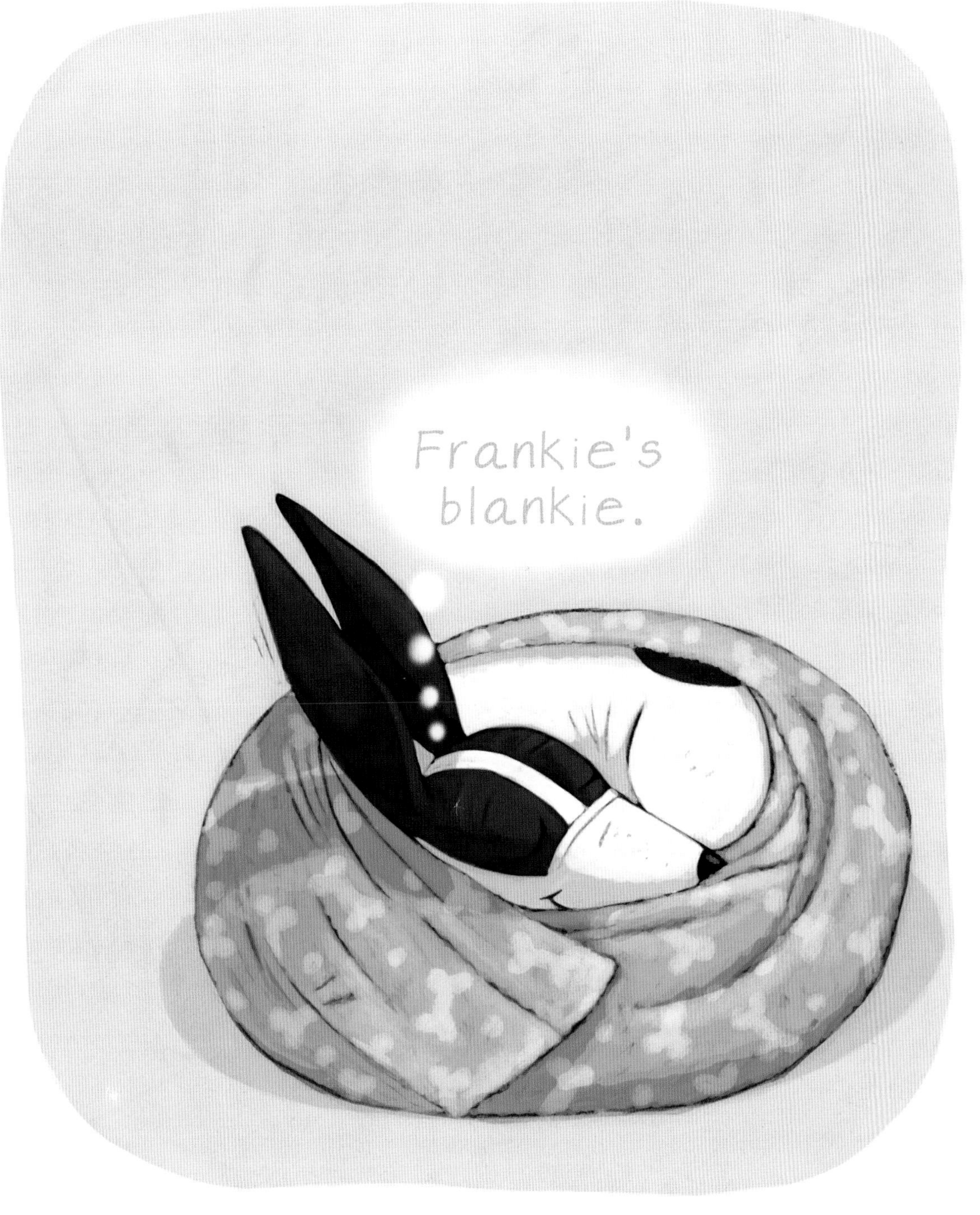
Frankie's
blankie.

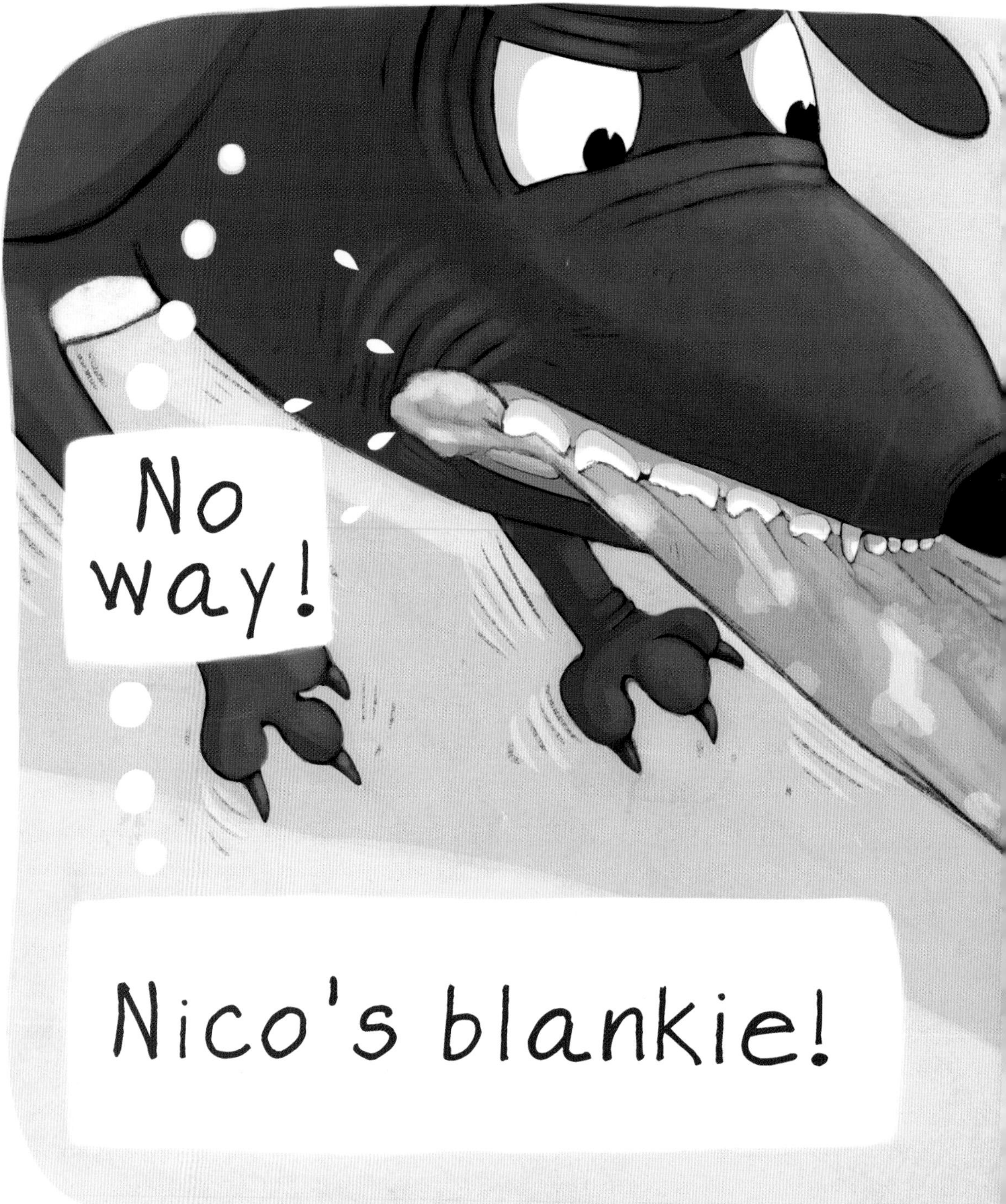
No way!
Nico's blankie!

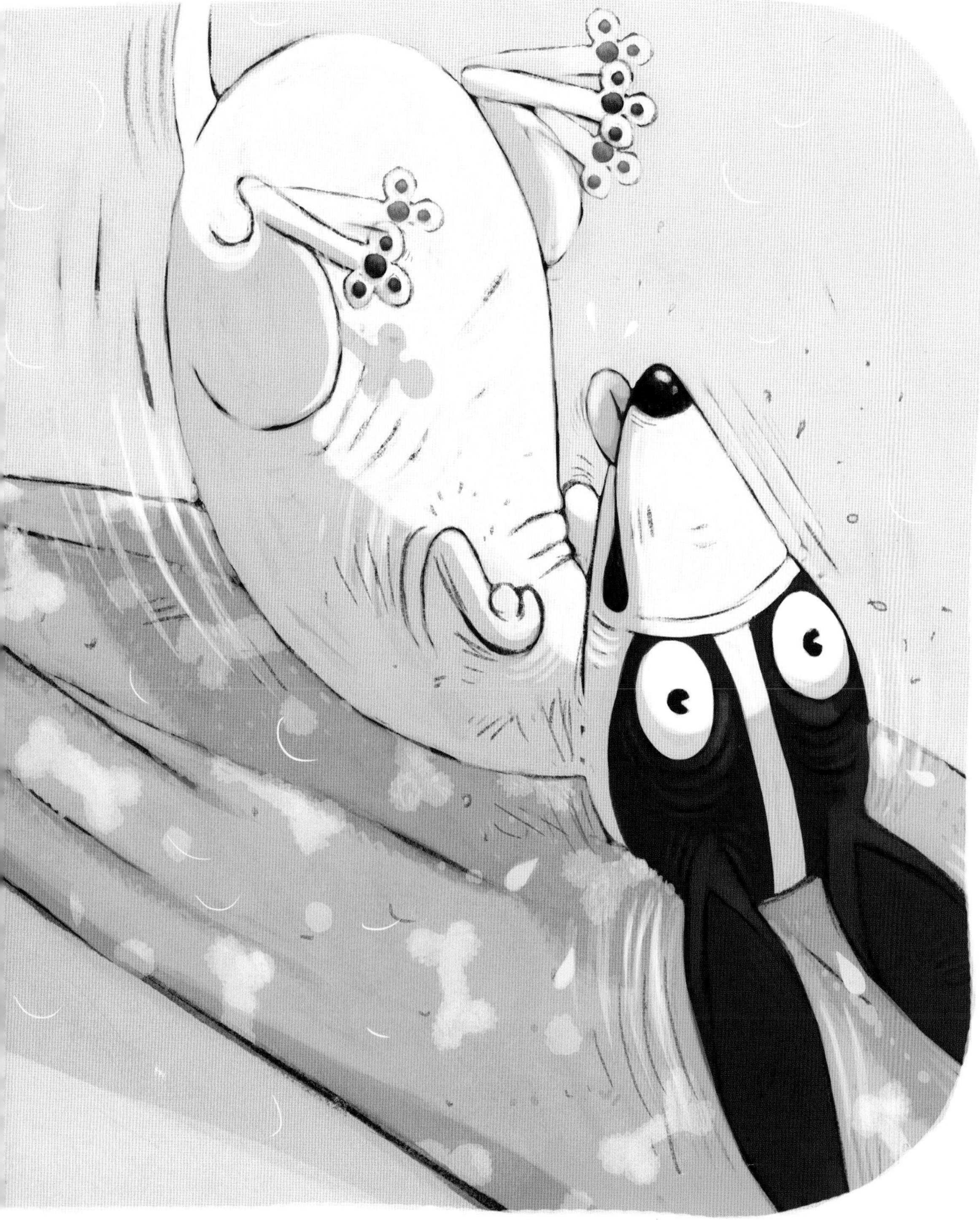

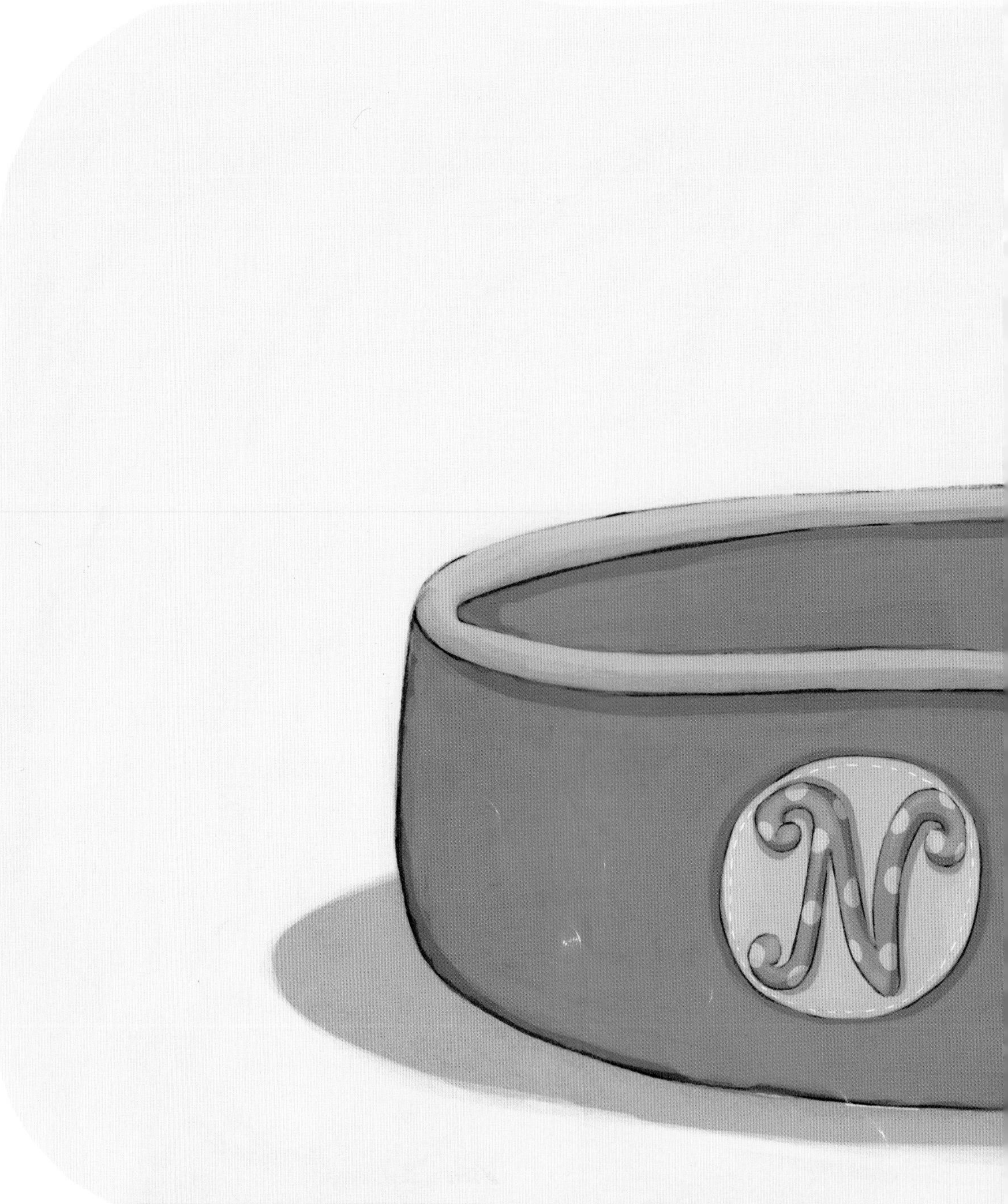
N

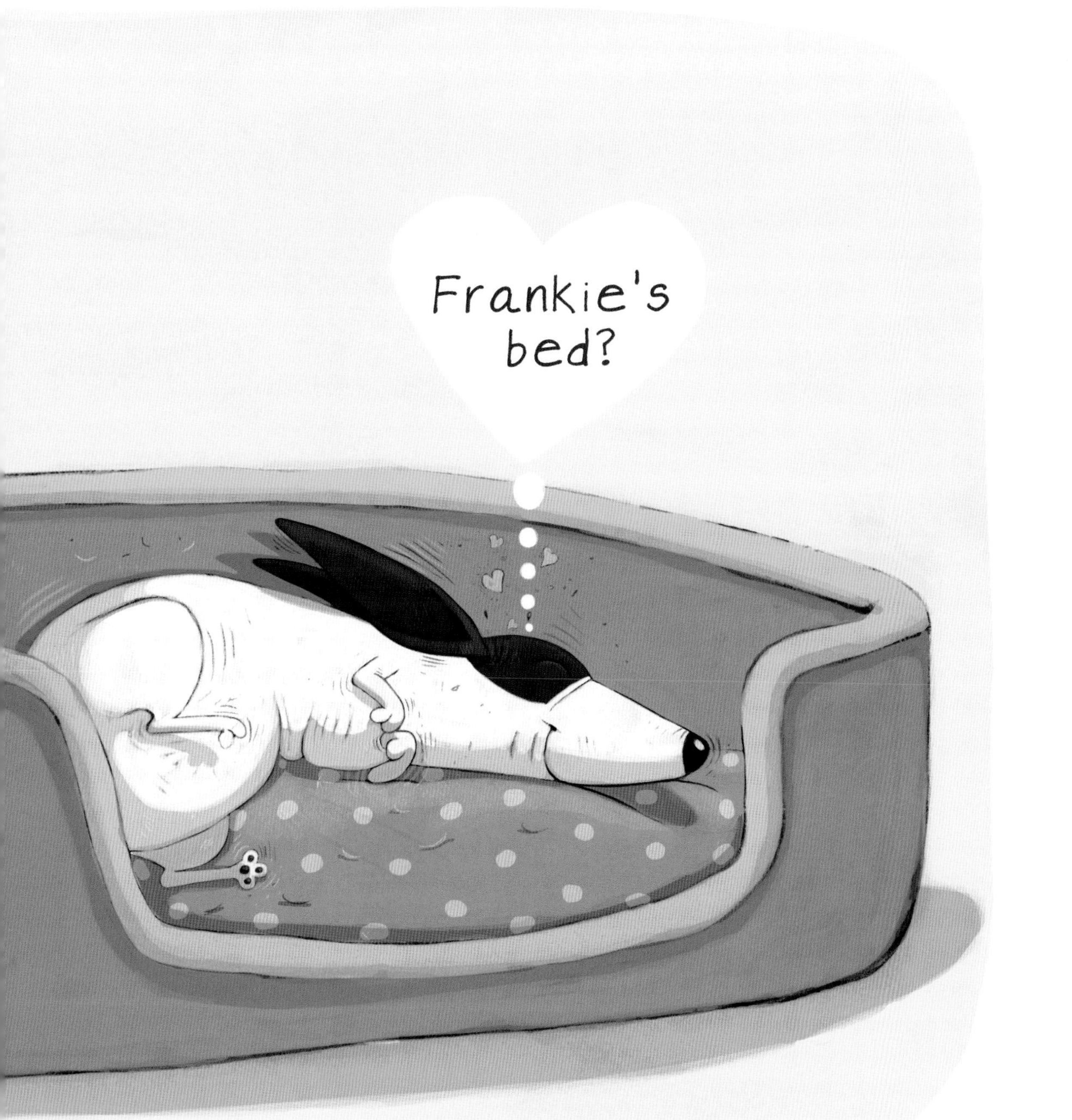
Frankie's
bed?

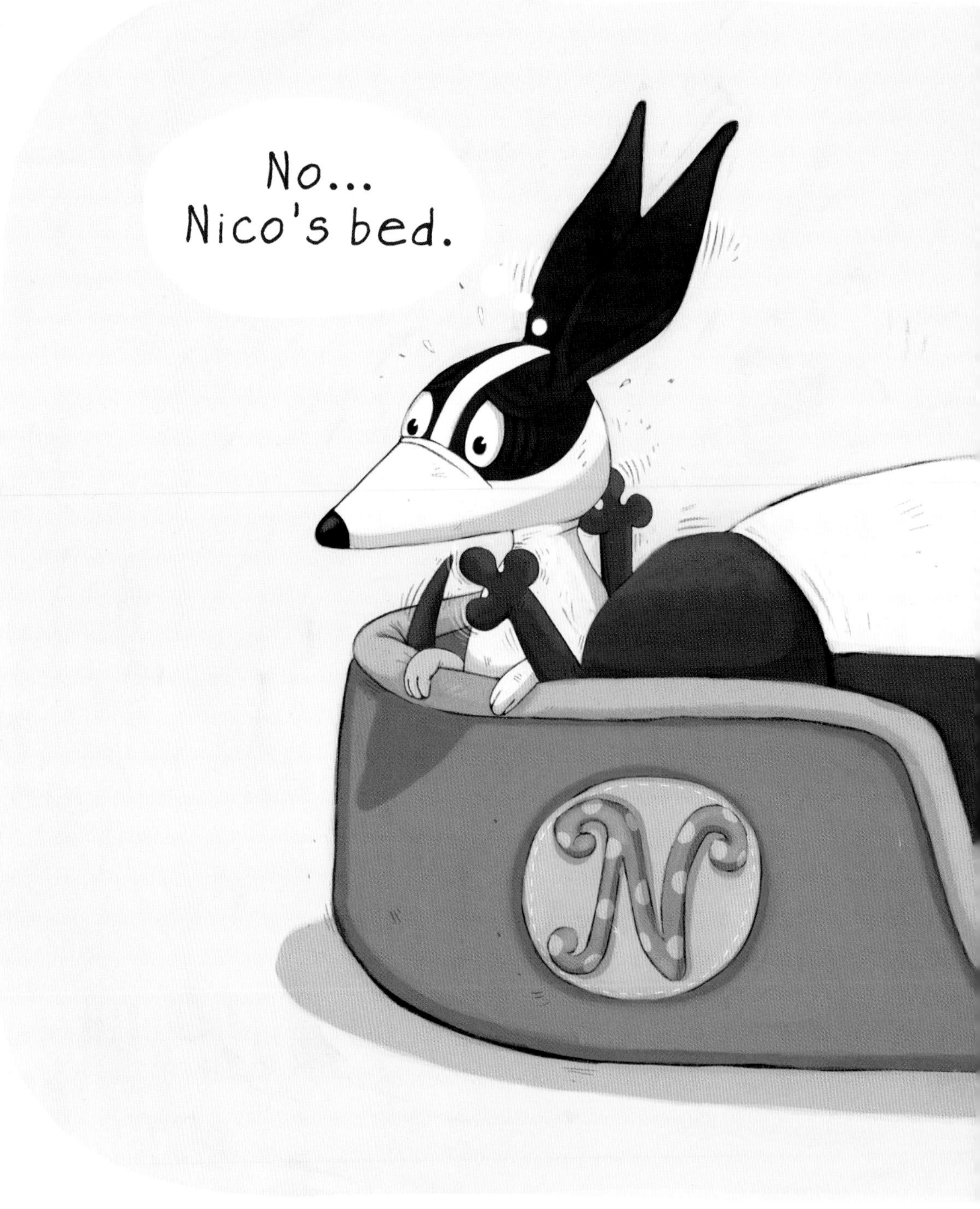
No...
Nico's bed.

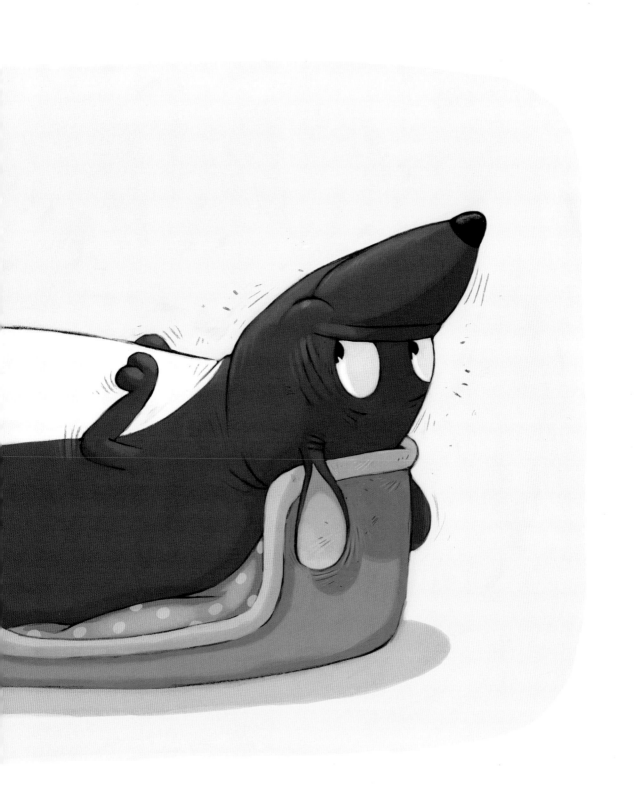

Poor Frankie.

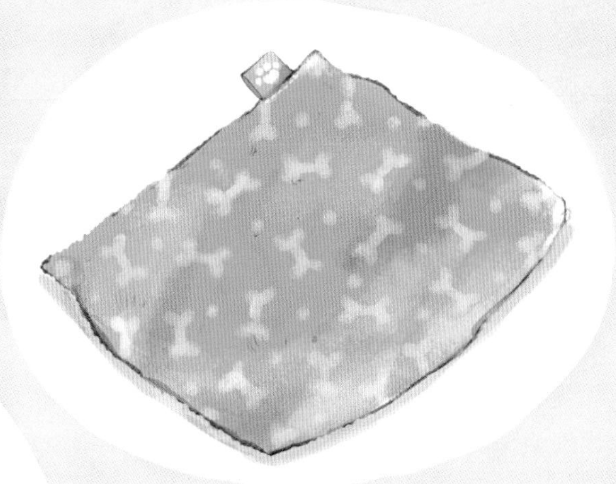

No blankie.

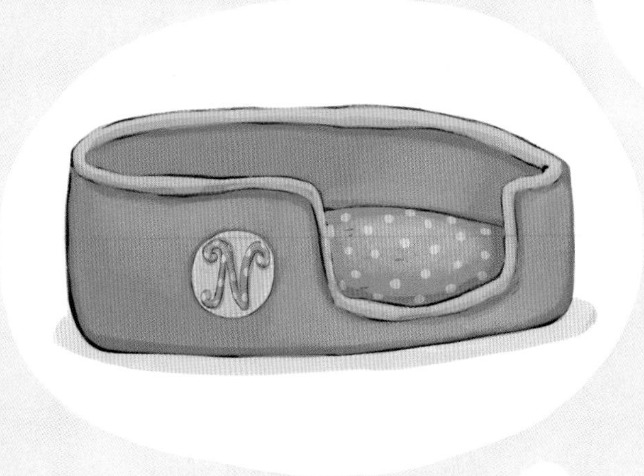

No bed.

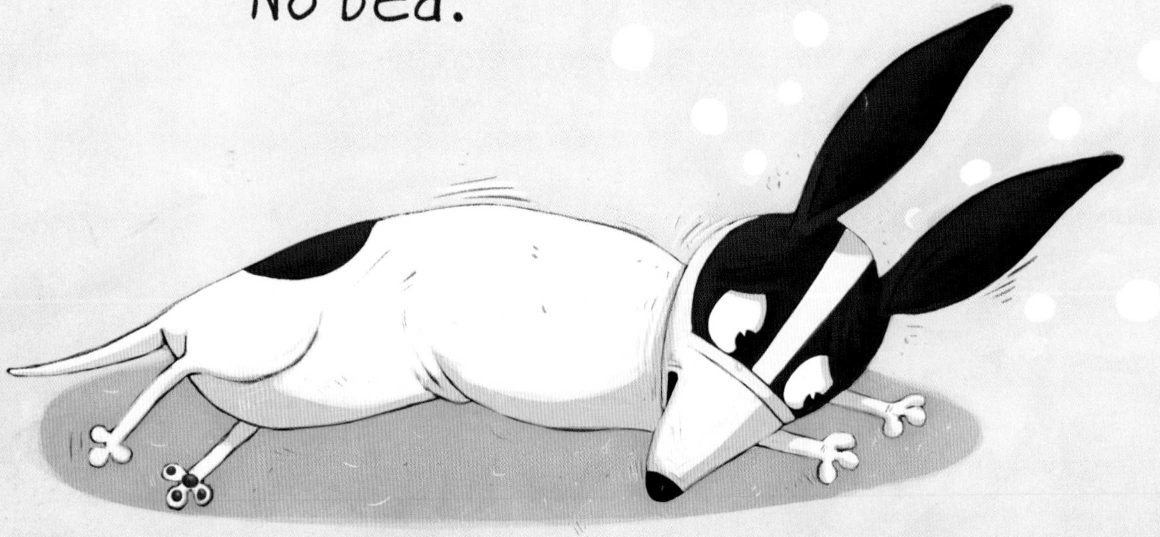

No rope.

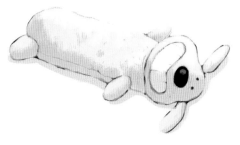

No puppy.

No bone.

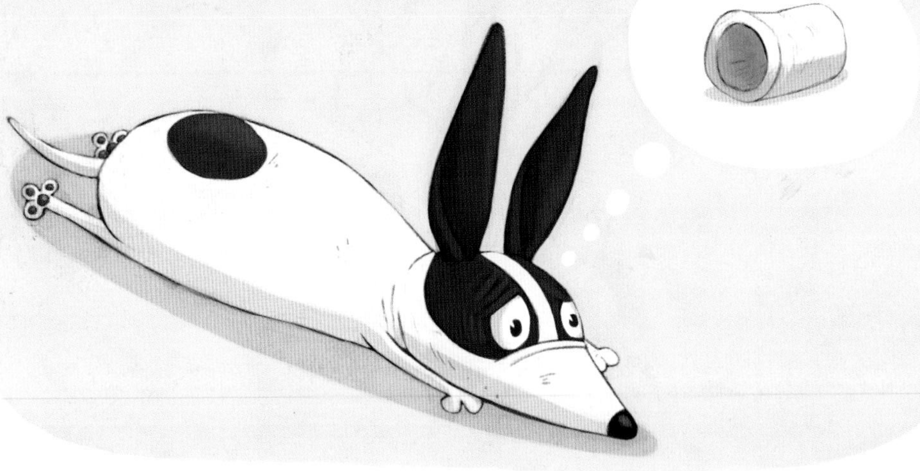

No ball.

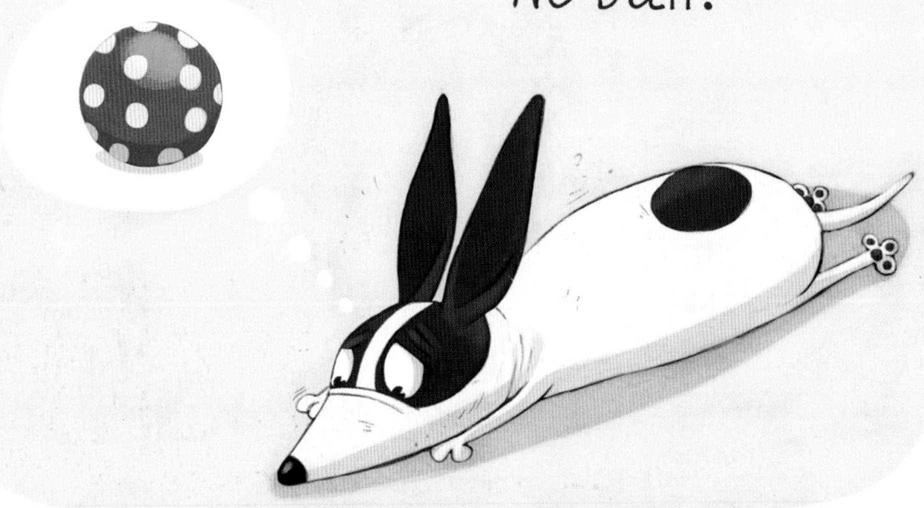

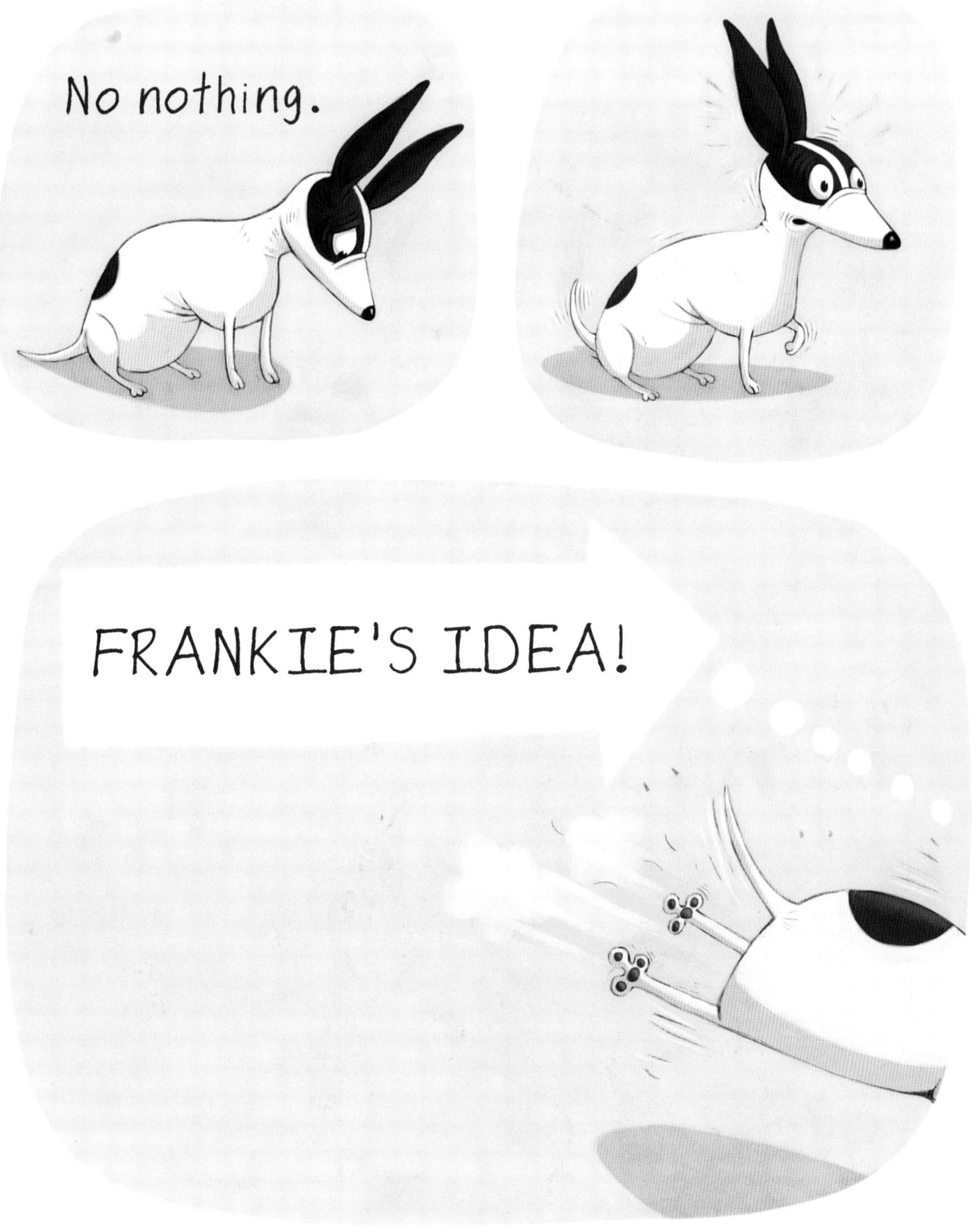
No nothing.
FRANKIE'S IDEA!

Frankie's...

ball.

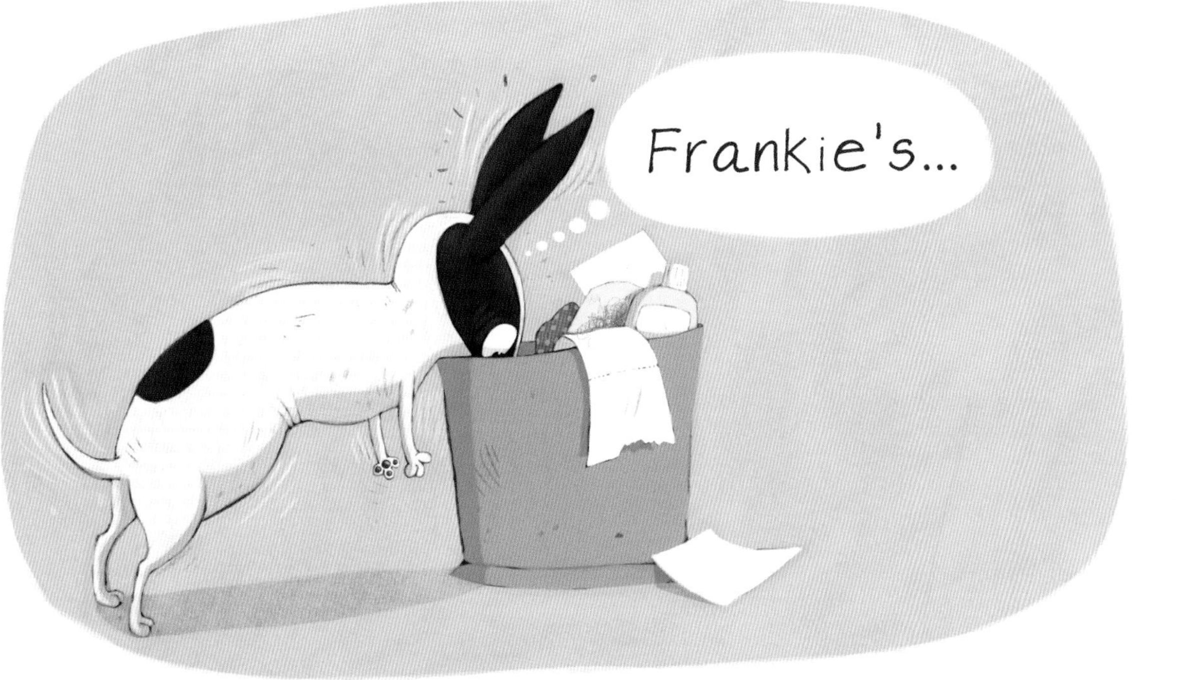
Frankie's...

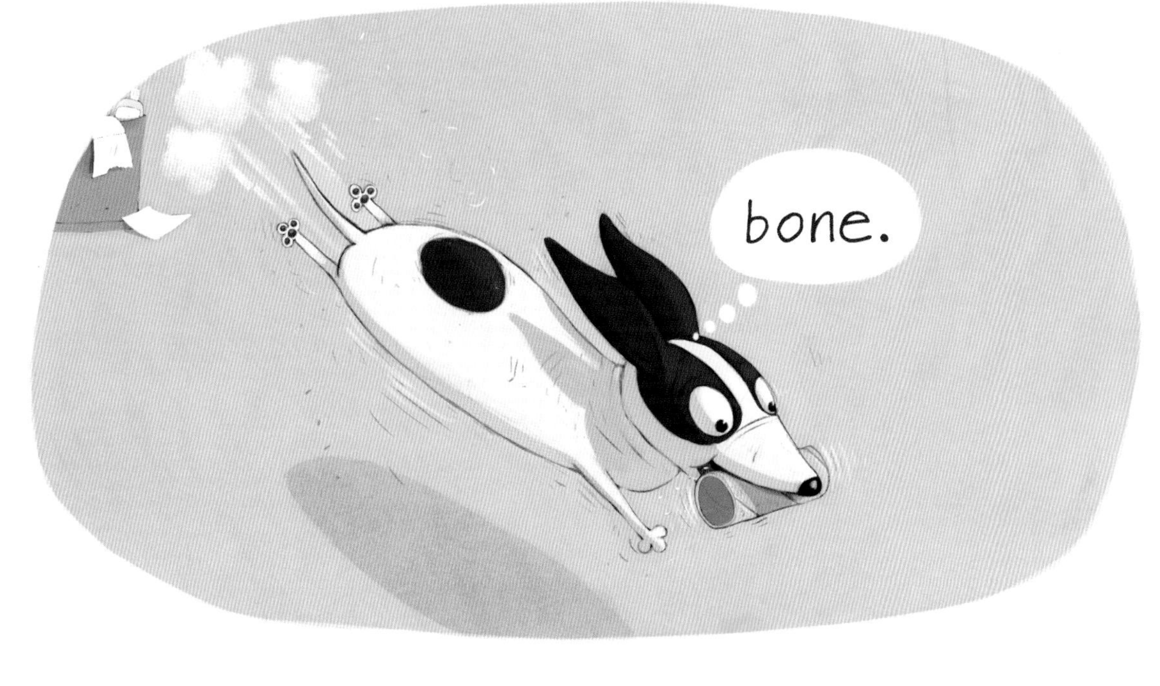
bone.

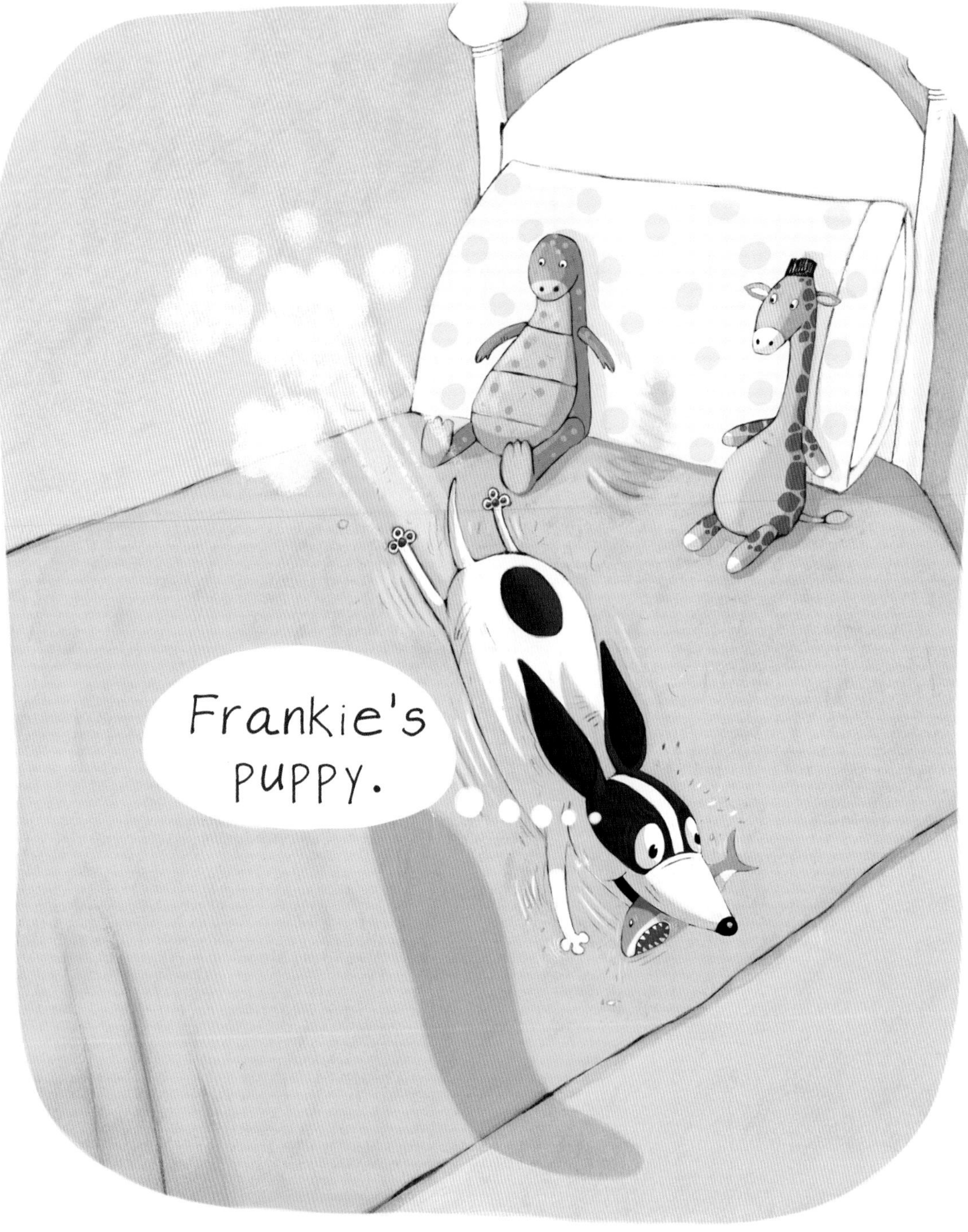
Frankie's puppy.

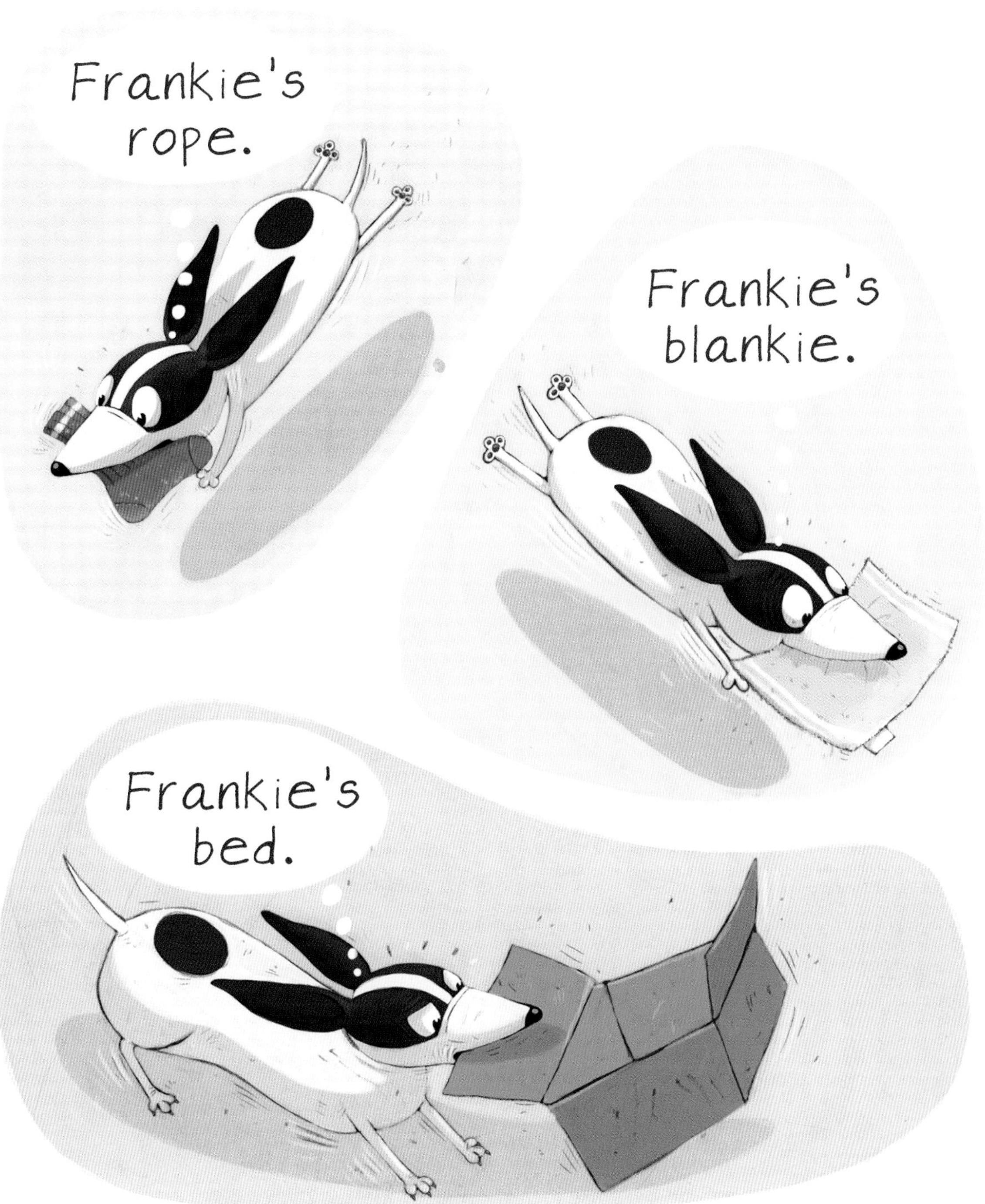
Frankie's rope.
Frankie's blankie.
Frankie's bed.

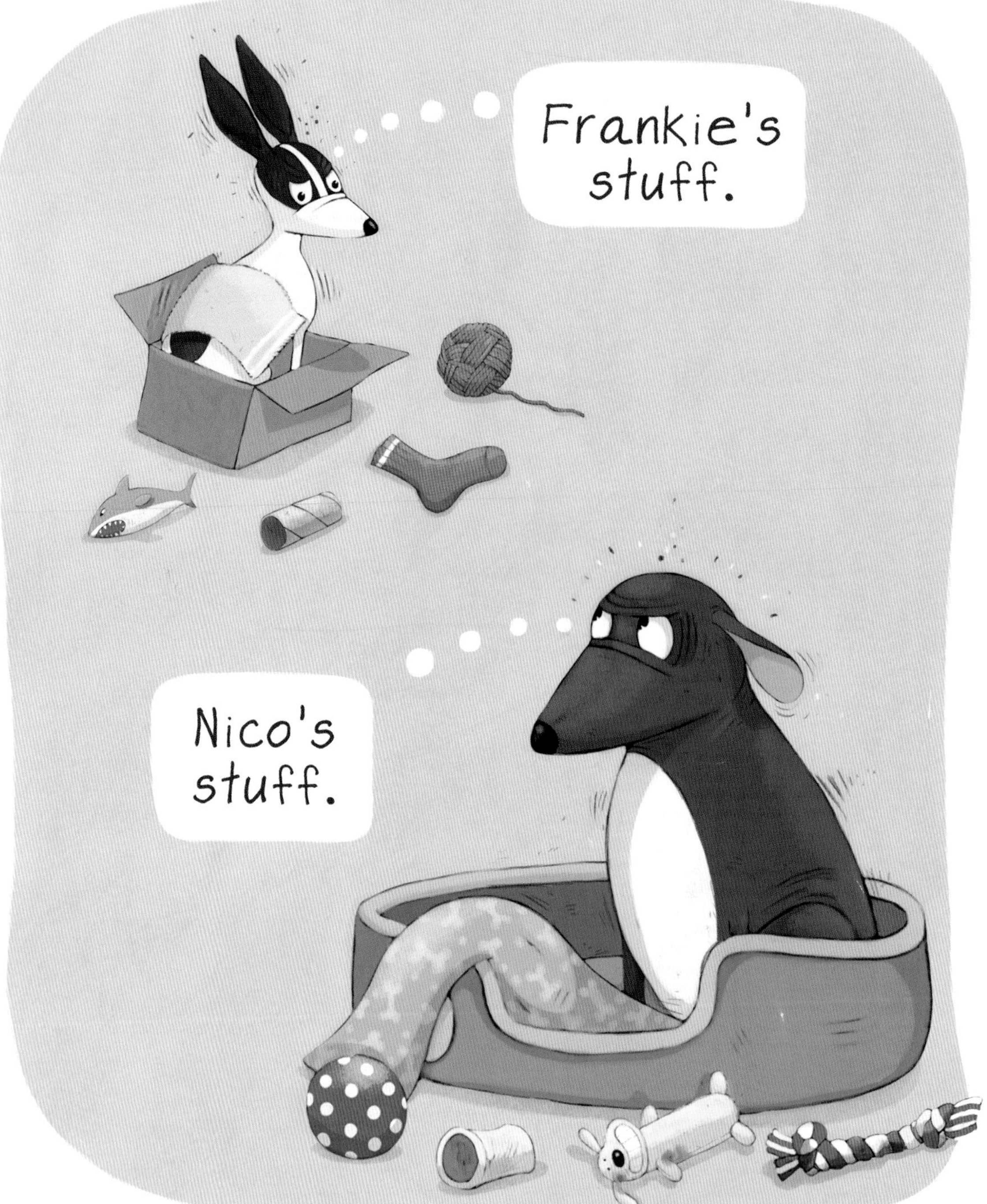
Frankie's stuff.
Nico's stuff.

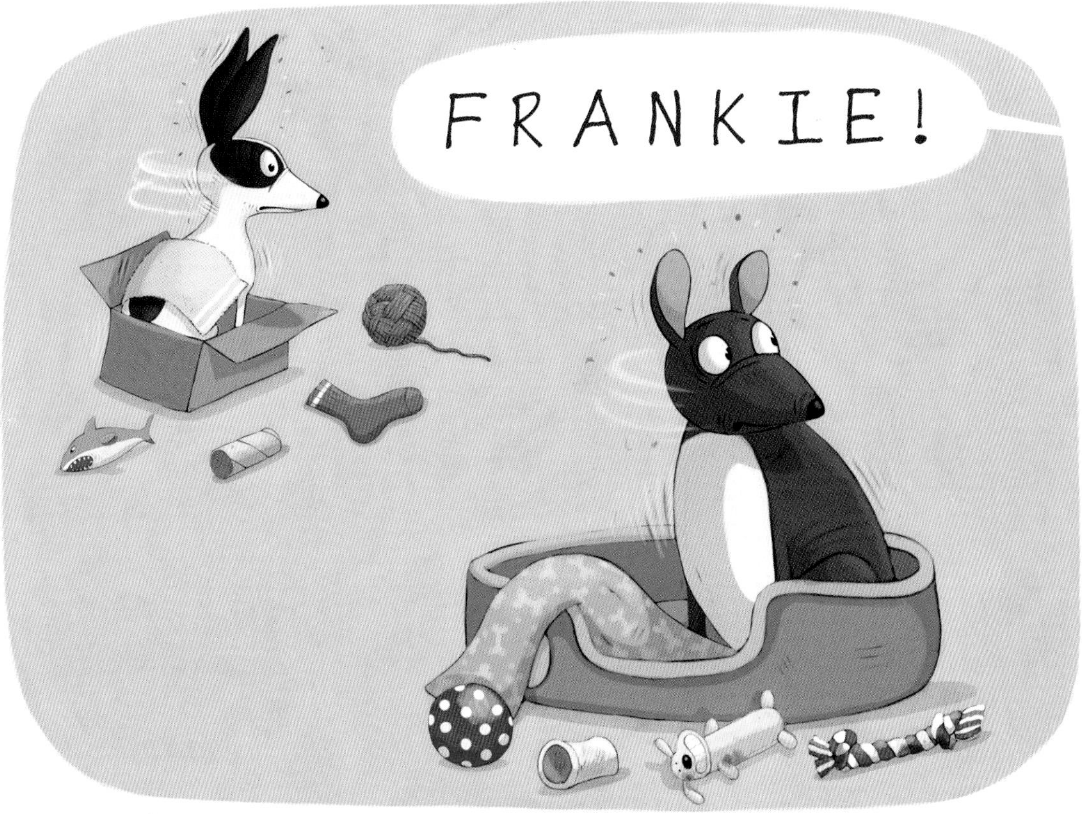
FRANKIE!

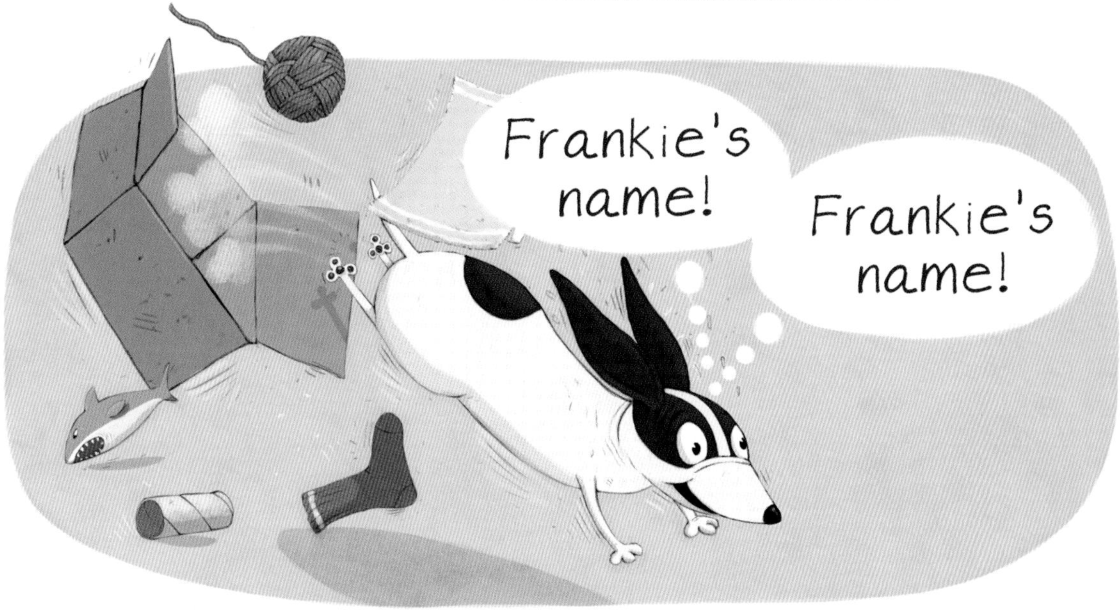
Frankie's name!
Frankie's name!

Frankie's stuff!

Frankie's
ball
bone
puppy
frog
log
rope
blankie
and bed!

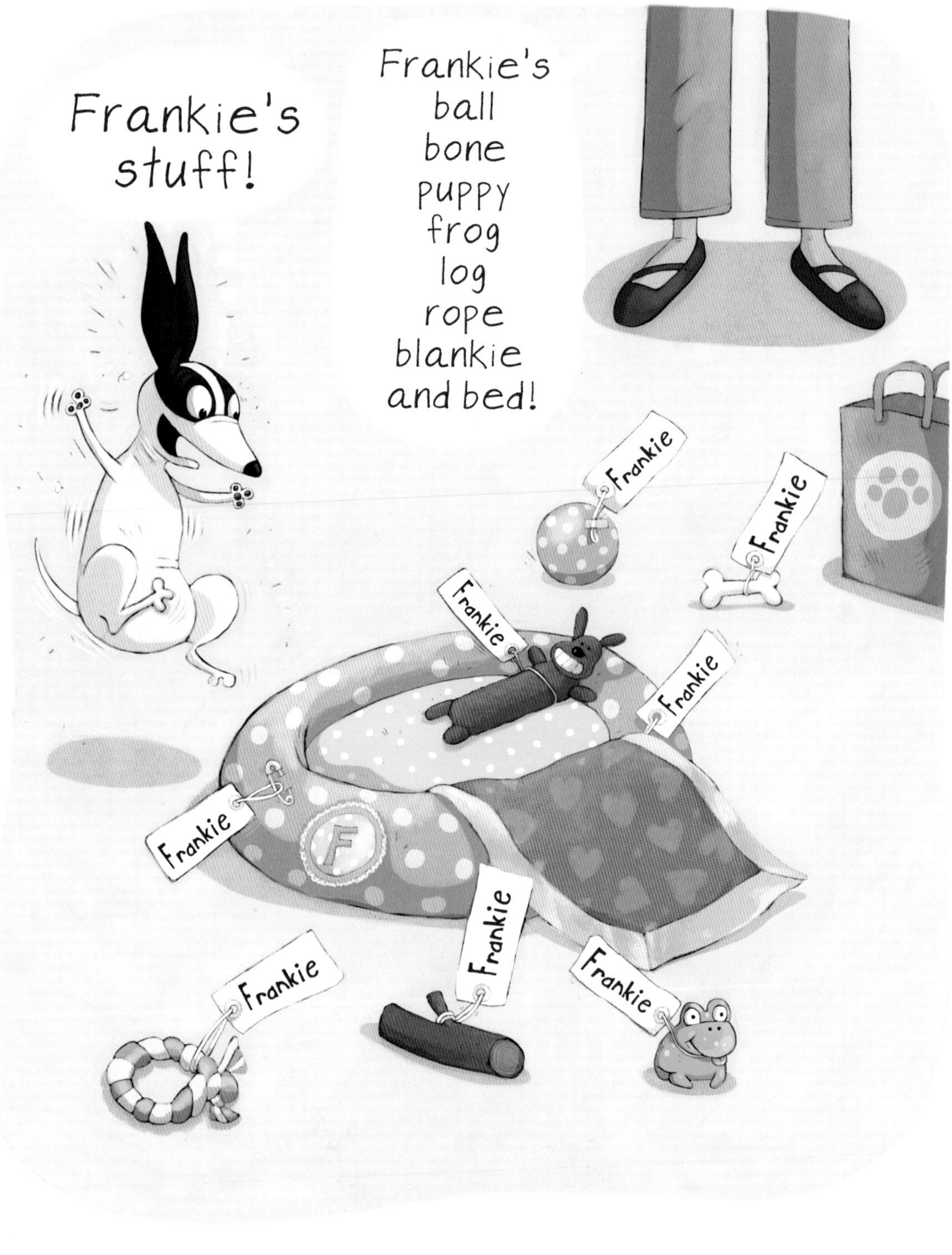
Frankie
Frankie
Frankie
Frankie
Frankie
Frankie
Frankie
Frankie

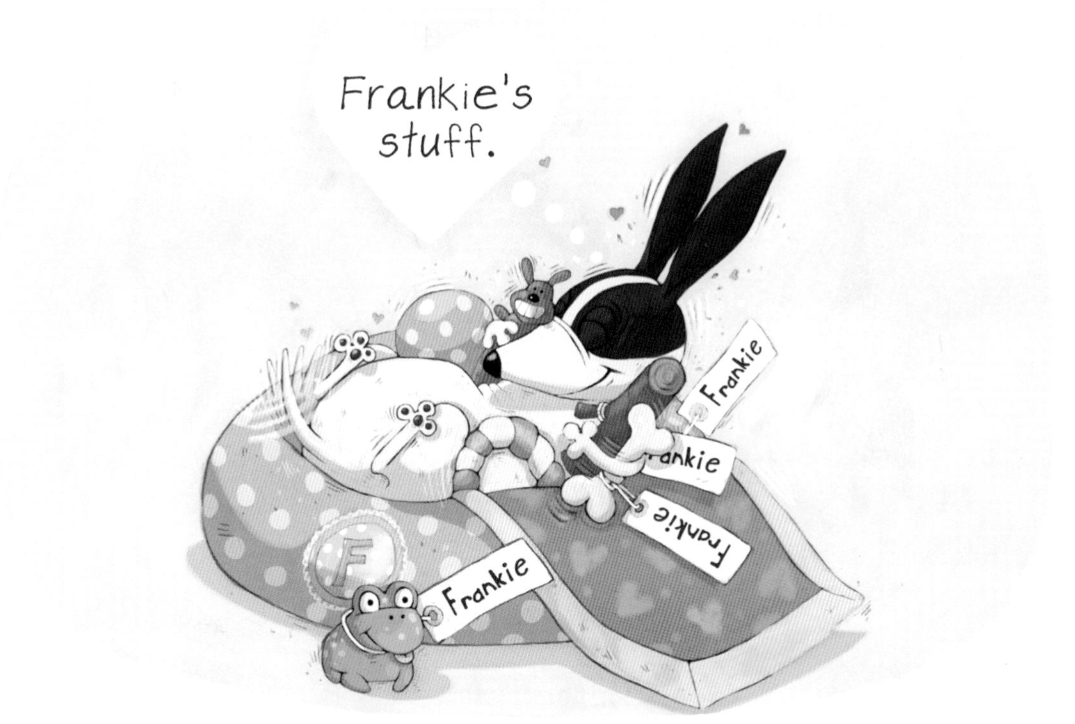
Frankie's stuff.
Frankie
Frankie
Frankie

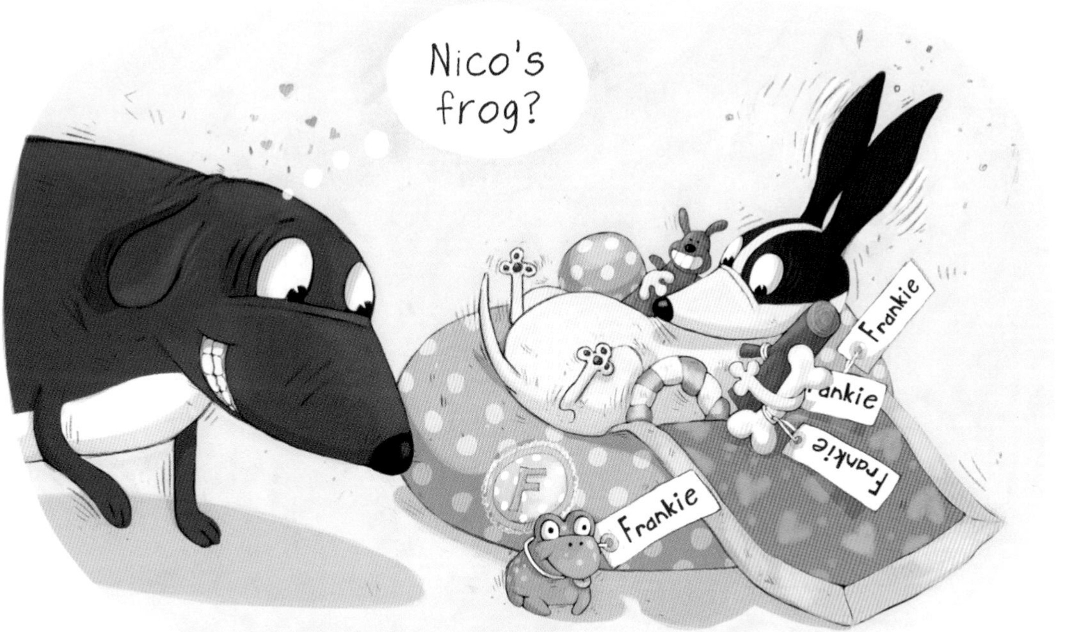
Nico's frog?
Frankie
Frankie
Frankie

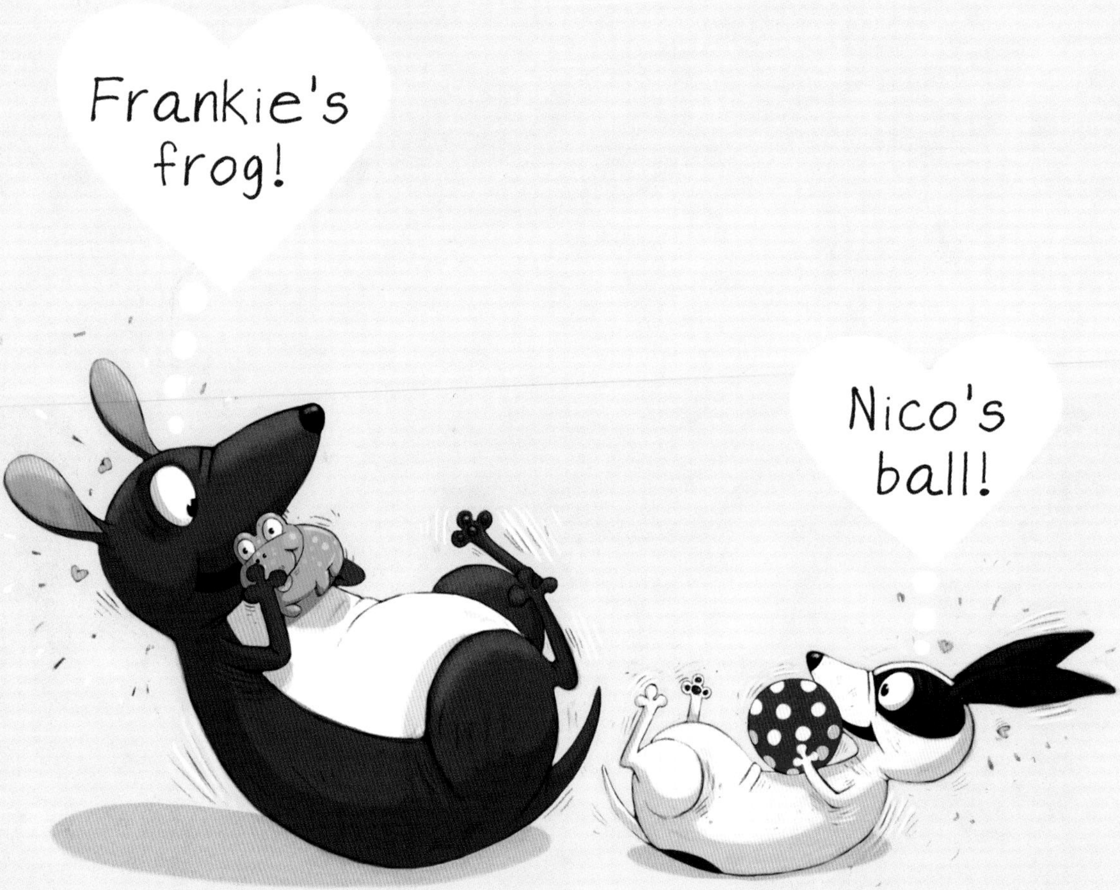
Frankie's frog!
Nico's ball!